For

For a dear Friend

A. Lovett 1997

Irmgard Schlater

A NEW BEGINNING

The Gift of Hope

Written and Edited by John P. Beilenson

Design by Michel Design
Photographs by Solomon M. Skolnick

PETER PAUPER PRESS, INC.
WHITE PLAINS · NEW YORK

Cover Design by Mullen & Katz
Cover photograph ©1994 Jill Sabella
Design by Michel Design
Photographs by Solomon M. Skolnick

Contents

INTRODUCTION

We can live "about 40 days without food," Hal Lindsey reminds us, "three days without water, about eight minutes without air . . . but only one second without hope." Hope "springs eternal" from our hearts. It is our lifeblood, animating our days.

In times of trouble, hope is the small, tenacious, utterly human part of us that looks unbelievingly at despair, that stiffens its lip at the prospect of suffering, and that laughs in the face of oppression. In difficult times, we must search out this hope and take action based on it, action that drives us through our fears and helps us to become happier, confident, peaceful people.

Begun with hope, each day is a new beginning. Each day is an opportunity to take risks, both large and small. Each day is a chance at a better life.

We have chosen the stories and the quotations included here because they have inspired us. Others have passed them on to us, and we would like to pass them on to you—each, as it were, a small gift of hope.

J.P.B.

Hope Reveals
Blessings in Disguise

Every cloud has a silver lining—if we are patient enough, if we are hopeful enough, to seek it out.

Once there was an old man who had a horse. One day the horse disappeared, and all his friends consoled him because of his loss. But the old man said, "How can you tell that it was not a lucky omen?"

After several months, the lost horse returned, bringing with him another fine horse. The old man's friends congratulated him, but he replied, "How can you tell that it was not a bad omen?"

By and by, his son began riding the horse as a hobby. One day he fell off and broke his leg very badly. Again, the old man's friends called to express their sorrow, and he replied, "How can you tell that it was not a good omen?"

Shortly thereafter, an order was given that all the young men be made to join the army to fight a great, far-off war. The crippled son, owing to his lameness, was, of course, spared.

Today's misfortune may turn out to be tomorrow's blessing.

To see a hillside white with dogwood bloom is to know a particular ecstasy of beauty, but to walk the gray Winter woods and find the buds which will resurrect that beauty in another May is to partake of continuity.

HAL BORLAND

True hope is swift and flies with swallow's wings;
Kings it makes gods, and meaner creatures kings.

WILLIAM SHAKESPEARE,
RICHARD III

Never let your head hang down. Never give up and sit down and grieve. Find another way. And don't pray when it rains if you don't pray when the sun shines.

SATCHEL PAIGE

In the spring I burned over a hundred acres till the earth was sere and black, and by mid-summer this space was clad in a fresher and more luxuriant green than the surrounding even. Shall man then despair? Is he not a sproutland too, after never so many searings and witherings?

HENRY D. THOREAU

I find I can't live without hope. Good things happen that we can't believe.

MADELEINE L'ENGLE

A misty morning does not signify a cloudy day.

ANCIENT PROVERB

Keep on going and the chances are you will stumble on something, perhaps when you are least expecting it. I have never heard of anyone stumbling on something sitting down.

CHARLES F. KETTERING

Some people are still unaware that reality contains unparalleled beauties. The fantastic and unexpected, the ever-changing and renewing is nowhere so exemplified as in real life itself.

BERENICE ABBOTT

We are continually faced by great opportunities brilliantly disguised as insolvable problems.

ANONYMOUS

Heroic Hope
Is Transformative

When all is lost, hope can transform even the worst disaster into a blessing, as this story of a farmer and the flood relates.

When the flood waters rose above the levee and seemed to keep rising, Steve Sandusky knew that the Iowa farm that had been in his family for five generations would be lost to the bank. Indeed, his fields were so deep in water that he could motor across most of them in a boat.

On the seventh night of the rain, the young farmer was holed up in his home, listening to his CB radio, when he heard a call from town that a nearby housing complex had been threatened. Many in the area responded, but Sandusky was the first there in his boat, braving the high winds and waters. When he got to the complex, the first floor was already under water, and Sheri Lovett, a local school teacher, was perched atop her kitchen counter, while her furniture floated nearby.

Sandusky helped Lovett to safety and with others managed to get the rest of the residents to shelter. When she dried off, Lovett offered to take Sandusky out to lunch to thank him. As things sometimes happen in small towns, it wasn't long before the two were dating regularly, and then became engaged. Less than a year after the flood, on a beautiful May day, the two were married.

"I thought I lost everything in that flood—my farm, my land, and my livelihood," said Sandusky. Subsequently, he used a government grant to go back to school to learn to become a medical technician. "But really, I have gained so much more. Sheri is the best thing that ever happened to me. Really, I've been blessed."

Hope lifts us above
even the worst disasters.

"Hope" is the thing with feathers—
That perches in the soul—
And sings the tune without the words—
And never stops—at all—

EMILY DICKINSON

Strong hope is a much greater stimulant of life than
any single realised joy could be.

NIETZSCHE

The golden opportunity you are seeking is in yourself.
It is not in your environment; it is not in luck or
chance, or the help of others; it is in yourself alone.

ORISON SWETT MARDEN

We should not let our fears hold us back from pursuing our hopes.

JOHN F. KENNEDY

Don't be afraid to take big steps. You can't cross a chasm in two small jumps.

DAVID LLOYD GEORGE

No one can go it alone. Somewhere along the way is the person who gives you that job, who has faith that you can make it. And everyone has something to work with, if only he will look for it.

GRACE GIL OLIVAREZ

You can't just sit there and wait for people to give you that golden dream, you've got to get out there and make it happen for yourself.

DIANA ROSS

We must do the things we think we cannot do.

ELEANOR ROOSEVELT

He who has hope has everything.

AMERICAN PROVERB

Hope Makes Laughter Possible

Just the prospect of a better day or a long-hoped-for event can put a smile on our faces, can bring us the small miracle of laughter, as this story from the Book of Genesis explains quite literally.

After God makes his covenant with Abraham, the Lord tells the old man that his wife Sarah will be blessed, that she shall have a son by Abraham, that "she will be a mother of nations." At this, Abraham, who is 99, falls on his face and laughs at the thought that he and his 90-year-old wife would have a child after all their years of hoping.

Later, in the desert, God sends three messengers to Abraham's tent to repeat this pledge. Sarah, who is hiding within the tent, also begins to laugh "within herself."

Of course, although they both laugh, this promise renews the hope of Abraham and Sarah. Soon enough, God makes sure that the old couple have a son. Fittingly, they name him Isaac, which is Hebrew for "he who laughs."

Hope can make miracles possible.

Against all hope, Abraham in hope believed and so
became the father of many nations . . .

ROMANS 4:18 (NIV)

Hope is itself a species of happiness, and, perhaps, the
chief happiness which this world affords . . .

SAMUEL JOHNSON

Dreams are wiser than men.

OMAHA INDIAN PROVERB

Every day is a new beginning . . . and a chance to
blow it.

CATHY GUISEWITE

He who laughs, lasts!

MARY PETTIBONE POOLE

Laughter is a tranquilizer with no side effects.

ARNOLD GLASOW

Moses dragged us for 40 years through the desert to bring us to the one place in the Middle East where there was no oil.

GOLDA MEIR

Hope is the feeling you have that the feeling you have isn't permanent.

JEAN KERR

Those who would enjoyment gain must find it in the purpose they pursue.

SARAH J. HALE

One cannot be always laughing at a man without now and then stumbling on something witty.

JANE AUSTEN

You grow up the day you have your first real laugh, at yourself.

ETHEL BARRYMORE

Laughter can be more satisfying than honor; more precious than money; more heart-cleansing than prayer.

HARRIET ROCHLIN

Hope for Tomorrow
Begins Today

The best way to build hope for tomorrow is to really live today. Hope flows naturally from an intense, in-the-moment connection to the people and world around us. An old Buddhist parable explains this quite well.

A traveler was chased by a tiger and ran until he came to the edge of a cliff. There, he caught hold of a thick vine and swung himself over the edge.

Above him, the tiger snarled. Below him, he heard another snarl, and behold, there was another tiger peering up at him. He was suspended midway between the two.

At that moment, two mice began to gnaw at the vine and were soon eating through it. The man, however, did not despair. In front of him on the cliffside, he saw a luscious bunch of ripe grapes. Holding onto the vine with one hand, he reached and picked a grape with the other.

"Um . . how delicious," he thought.

Even in the most difficult circumstances, hope can be plucked from the little things around us.

The future is in the present. Look and see for yourself.

THICH NHAT HANH

The creative power of our thoughts, words and actions gives form to the energy in the universe. Life is energy. Breath is energy. Thought is energy. An unlimited supply of energy is all around us and is ours to shape as we will.

SUSAN TAYLOR

Woe to the man whose heart has not learned while young to hope, to love—and to put its trust in life.

JOSEPH CONRAD

We build our temples for tomorrow, strong as we know how, and we stand on top of the mountain, free within ourselves.

LANGSTON HUGHES

Just as despair can come to one only from other human beings, hope, too, can be given to one only by other human beings.

ELIE WIESEL

With a garden there is hope.

GRACE FIRTH

If you are wise, you will mingle one thing with
the other, not hoping without doubt, not doubting
without hope.

SENECA

The natural flights of the human mind are not from
pleasure to pleasure, but from hope to hope.

SAMUEL JOHNSON

I steer my bark with hope in the head, leaving
fear astern.

THOMAS JEFFERSON

You must begin wherever you are.

JACK BOLAND

Hope Is a Light
in the Darkest Night

Anyone can have hope, and that hope, lifted for others to see, can be an inspiration to all. A South African folk tale describes this lesson.

Long ago, the sky was pitch black at night, but people learned in time to make fires to light up the darkness.

One night, a young girl, warming herself by a wood fire, was playing with the ashes. She took them in her hands and threw them up to see how pretty they were when they floated in the air. As they floated away, she put more wood on the fire and stirred the blaze with a stick. Bright sparks flew everywhere and wafted up and through the ashes, high into the night. They hung in the air and made a bright road across the sky, looking like silver and diamonds.

And there the road is to this day. Some call it the Milky Way; some call it the Stars' Road. But no matter what you call it, it is a path made many, many years ago by a young girl who threw the bright sparks of her fire high up into the sky to make a road in the darkness.

Hope lights the path for others to follow.

Not all who seem to fail have failed indeed,
Not all who fail have therefore worked in vain.
There is no failure for the good and brave.

ARCHBISHOP FRENCH

Neither the lords nor the shogun can be depended
upon [to save the country], and so our only hope lies
in grass-roots heroes.

YOSHIDA SHOIN

But, "I can't," is a great barrier in the way. I hope it
will soon be removed, and "I will," resume its place.

MARIA W. STEWART

While there's life, there's hope.

CICERO

As long as there is one upright man, as long as there is one compassionate woman, the contagion may spread and the scene is not desolate. Hope is the thing that is left us in a bad time.

E. B. WHITE

Not westward, but eastward seek the coming of the light.

DAKOTA INDIAN PROVERB

Nothing can dim the light which shines from within.

MAYA ANGELOU

Light tomorrow with today.

ELIZABETH BARRETT BROWNING

Hope Grows Strongest in the Most Desperate Conditions

The most beautiful examples of hope often spring from our most difficult days, in the harshest of times. As a symbol of resilient hope, Henry David Thoreau directs us to the simple water lily.

Again I [discover the] scent [of] the white water-lily, and a season I had waited for is arrived. It is the emblem of purity and its scent suggests it. Growing in the stagnant and muddy water, it bursts so pure and fair to the eye and so sweet to the scent, as if to show what purity and sweetness reside in, and can be extracted from, the slime and muck of earth. What confirmation of our hopes is in the fragrance of the water-lily! I shall not soon despair the world of it.

Hope blooms even in the
humblest places.

The human body experiences a powerful gravitational pull in the direction of hope. That is why the patient's hopes are the physician's secret weapon. They are the hidden ingredients in any prescription.

NORMAN COUSINS

Inspiration is 95% nature and silence.

ALICE WALKER

All my hope on God is founded;
He doth still my trust renew,
Me through change and chance he guideth,
Only good and only true.
God unknown,
He alone
Calls my heart to be his own.

ROBERT BRIDGES

In all things it is better to hope than to despair.

JOHANN WOLFGANG VON GOETHE

Birds sing after a storm, why shouldn't we?

ROSE FITZGERALD KENNEDY

All this drudgery will kill me if once in a while I cannot hope something, for somebody! If I cannot sometimes see a bird fly and wave my hand to it.

WILLA CATHER

I am thankful for the adversities which have crossed my path and taught me tolerance, perseverance, self-control and some other virtues I might never have known.

ANONYMOUS

Hope Springs Eternal

While many of us live in urban or suburban settings, we are not many generations removed from a more rural life. Perhaps this is why we still derive hope from the coming of Spring and Autumn (and why so many of our holidays coincide with the times for planting and harvest). The following Penobscot myth evokes this ancient spirit, which still lives with us today.

Many years ago, Natarwunsum, helper to the great teacher Klose-kur-beh, married a beautiful maiden. She soon conceived and, together, they began to raise a large family. The maid was thus called Neegaroose, or First Mother, and she loved her children very much.

After a number of years, and having many more children, Neegaroose inexplicably grew despondent. One

day, hoping to raise her spirits, Natarwunsum asked
her to come outside and watch the beautiful sun as it
set. Neegaroose consented, and as they stood there
together, seven of their little children came up and
said, "We are in hunger and night will soon come;
where is the food?" The First Mother cried seven tears,
and said, "Hold your peace little ones, in seven moons
you shall be filled and shall hunger no more." When
Natarwunsum asked what he could do to help, she
said directly, "You must take a stone implement and
kill me."

Now, Natarwunsum loved Neegaroose very much and
didn't know what to do, so he traveled up north to
where Klose-kur-beh lived and asked him for advice.
The great teacher said Natarwunsum must do what
Neegaroose asked.

When Natarwunsum returned, Neegaroose told him
that after he killed her, he must drag her body over a

large open space of land until all her flesh was worn away. The First Mother continued, "After all this is done, wait seven moons and come back, and gather all that you find and eat it, but not all of it—save some to put in the land again."

So Natarwunsum did as he was told, and did not return to the spot until seven moons had passed. He found the ground covered with tall, golden plants, and he tasted their sweet fruit and called it "skarmoonal" or corn. And following Neegaroose's instructions, he shared it with the others and saved some kernels to put back in the ground. In this way, all of the people had enough to eat, and the spirit of the First Mother was renewed every seven months, generation after generation.

From love and sacrifice, hope is reborn each day and each season.

Hope springs eternal in the human breast . . .

ALEXANDER POPE

Hope works in these ways: it looks for the good in people instead of harping on the worst; it discovers what can be done instead of grumbling about what cannot; it regards problems, large or small, as opportunities; it pushes ahead when it would be easy to quit; it "lights a candle" instead of "cursing the darkness."

For hope grew round me, like the twining vine,
And fruits, and foliage, not my own, seemed mine.

SAMUEL TAYLOR COLERIDGE

It is never too late to be what you might have become.

GEORGE ELIOT

The hopeful man sees success where others see failure, sunshine where others see shadows and storm.

O. S. MARDEN

All things are possible until they are proved impossible—even the impossible may only be so, as of now.

PEARL S. BUCK

Love the moment, and the energy of that moment will spread beyond all boundaries.

CORITA KENT

In the province of the mind, what one believes to be true either is true or becomes true.

JOHN LILLY

Hope is a flatterer, but the most upright of all parasites; for she frequents the poor man's huts, as well as the palace of his superior.

WILLIAM SHENSTONE

It is not the variegated colors, the cheerful sounds, and the warm breezes which enliven us so much in Spring; it is the quiet prophetic spirit of endless hope, a presentiment of many happy days, the anticipation of higher everlasting blossoms and fruits, and the secret sympathy with the world that is developing itself.

MARTIN OPITZ

One needs something to believe in, something for which one can have whole-hearted enthusiasm. One needs to feel that one's life has meaning, that one is needed in this world.

HANNAH SENESH

Hope Is the Mainstay of Perseverance

Hope gives us the courage to go on, to move forward even when our lives don't feel worth living. In the case of a school teacher afflicted with kidney failure, hope, in fact, made a normal, productive life possible.

When Agnes Stovel, an elementary school teacher in Raleigh, North Carolina, developed pneumonia, she lost the normal functioning of her kidneys. Not one to give up easily, she began treatment that required her to spend many evenings in a clinic, hooked up to a dialysis machine. She told no one at her school, and quietly signed up for the kidney transplant program at a nearby hospital.

With hundreds of others on the list, Stovel waited for months, continuing not only her dialysis treatment, but her regular work at school. Then one day, the phone rang, and the hospital told her they had a kidney for her.

"I had been praying for a kidney every night," recalls Stovel. "I said, 'Lord, I know that there are many who are in great need, and I will understand if you give it to them, but in your majesty and power, if there's one around, I want it.'"

The next day, Stovel went in for the operation, and six weeks later she was back on the job, leading her students not only with her intelligence and skills, but by example as well.

One cannot live without hope.

He is the best physician who is the most ingenious inspirer of hope.

SAMUEL TAYLOR COLERIDGE

Hope is patience with the lamp lit.

TERTULLIAN

Every thing that is done in the world is done by hope.

MARTIN LUTHER

Everyone who is successful must have dreamed of something.

MARICOPA INDIAN PROVERB

Success seems to be largely a matter of hanging on after others have let go.

WILLIAM FEATHER

There are no hopeless situations; there are only men who have grown hopeless about them.

CLARE BOOTHE LUCE

It is a long lane that has no turning.

OLD SAYING

When you get to the end of your rope, tie a knot and hang on.

ANONYMOUS

The men who build the future are those who know that greater things are yet to come, and that they themselves will help bring them about. Their minds are illumined by the blazing sun of hope. They never stop to doubt. They haven't time.

MELVIN J. EVANS

The difference between the impossible and the possible lies in a person's determination.

TOMMY LASORDA

I might have been born in a hovel, but I determined to travel with the wind and stars.

JACQUELINE COCHRAN

Sow the Seeds of Hope

We must first plant the seeds of hope through-out our lives. We must treat ourselves and others compassionately and optimistically. We must spread kind words and actions like so many seeds in a field. We must take the time to support and serve our family and friends, as well as strangers. If we keep up this "planting," these seeds will grow. We will find ourselves surrounded by joy and love and hope. Here is a short list of hopeful "seeds" one might sow.

🌱 Set aside five minutes each morning to say a meditation or prayer.

🌱 Hug all your loved ones at least once a day.

🌱 If you have children, set aside one night a week for

you and your spouse to go out on a date.

&o When no one else is there, plant bulbs around your house in the Autumn, and let everyone enjoy the miracle in the Spring.

&o Do someone else's chores around the house and don't tell them.

&o On your birthday, give other people gifts and tell them why you love and care for them.

Hope is contagious. Spread it around.

Every fire is the same size when it starts.

SENECA INDIAN PROVERB

To travel hopefully is better than to arrive.

SIR JAMES JEANS

First thoughts have tremendous energy. It is the way the mind first flashes on something. The internal censor usually squelches them, so we live in the realm of second and third thoughts, thoughts on thoughts.

NATALIE GOLDBERG

Every small, positive change we can make in ourselves repays us in confidence in the future.

ALICE WALKER

To me real courage is metaphysical and has to do with keeping one's passion for life intact, one's curiosity at full stretch, when one is daily hemmed in by death, disease, and lesser mayhems of the heart.

DIANE ACKERMAN

Hope is an echo, hope ties itself yonder, yonder.

CARL SANDBURG

None of us suddenly becomes something overnight. The preparations have been in the making for a lifetime.

GAIL GODWIN

As I started looking, I found more and more.

VALERIE STEELE

Each person has an ideal, a hope, a dream of some sort which represents his soul. In the long light of eternity this seed of the future is all that matters! We must find this seed no matter how small it is; we must give to it the warmth of love, the light of understanding and the water of encouragement. We must learn to deal with people as they are—not as we wish them to be. We must study the moral values which shape our thinking, arouse our emotions and guide our conduct. We must get acquainted with our inner stream and find out what's going on in our heads and hearts. We must put an end to blind, instinctive, sensory thought and feeling. We must take time to be human.

COLBY DORR DAM